ELLIE AND LUMP'S VERY BUSY DAY

For John, who was in
at the beginning - D.C.

For Anna - B.P.

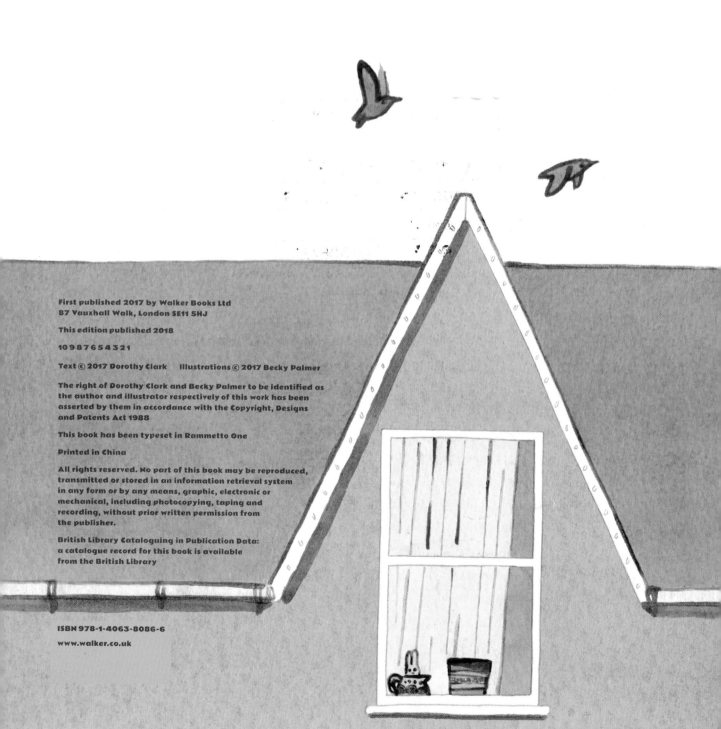

First published 2017 by Walker Books Ltd
87 Vauxhall Walk, London SE11 5HJ

This edition published 2018

10 9 8 7 6 5 4 3 2 1

Text © 2017 Dorothy Clark   Illustrations © 2017 Becky Palmer

The right of Dorothy Clark and Becky Palmer to be identified as
the author and illustrator respectively of this work has been
asserted by them in accordance with the Copyright, Designs
and Patents Act 1988

This book has been typeset in Rammetto One

Printed in China

British Library Cataloguing in Publication Data:
a catalogue record for this book is available
from the British Library

ISBN 978-1-4063-8086-6

www.walker.co.uk

ELLIE AND LUMP'S
VERY BUSY
DAY

DOROTHY CLARK

illustrated by
BECKY PALMER

WALKER BOOKS
AND SUBSIDIARIES

LONDON · BOSTON · SYDNEY · AUCKLAND

We're under the covers.
Giggle snort giggle,
Listening to the clock.

Tick tock!

Mum says, "It's time to get up, Ellie and Lump!"

"We're up!"
Squeak boing!
Squeak boing boing!

Bouncing on the bed.
"Hooray!"

RAT-A-TAT-TAT!
There's someone
at the door.

"Post for Dad,
not for us,"
says Mum.

We're cracking our eggs.
Split splat! Split splat!

We're going into town.

"Anoraks on!" says Mum.

Rustle ... rustle...

Zzzip! Zzzip!

PoP! PoP!

Down the path we go.
CRUNCH! CRUNCH!
"Wait for me,
Ellie and
Lump!"

"Stand still!" Mum says as we
wriggle wriggle twist
and the traffic *zoom zoom*
rushes by.

Ding ding! HONK! Beep!

"Safe to cross now," says Mum.

So we skip STOMP skip ...

to the shops!

We're buying ribbons and balloons, sparkly paper and CAKE!

Our trolley rattles.
Clink clank clonk!

Ellie says, "I want

Whizz!

"It's my turn

Whoosh!

"Yippeee

to push it first!"

Crash!

...now!" says Lump.

Clunk!

...e e!"

Then...

Home by the pet shop.
Tweet! WUFF! Miaow!

Polly parrot says, "See you again!"

We're back now.
CRUNCH!
  CRUNCH!
Up the path
we go.

It's time for juice.
Slurp ... slurp...
Splish SPLASH!
"I've spilt mine!"
says Ellie.

We're blowing up balloons.
Puff! Puff! Puff!

Sticking up stars.
Stickety-stick!

And we're putting on our fancy dress!

Stretch and *squeeze...*

"Ellie, your ears
are sticking out!"
"So are yours, Lump!"

RAT-A-TAT-TAT!
Ding dong!
goes the door.

"Everyone's almost here!" says Mum.

Shh shh shh shh...
Quietly now – we're all hiding.

Everyone shouts, "Whoo-hoo! Hip hip HOORAY!"

There's jelly for tea.
Flip flop! Flip squelch!
Cake to cut.

Balloons to burst.
BANG! BANG!

The party is over.

"GOODBYE!"

"GOODBYE!"

Time for us to get warm indoors.

"What a BUSY day!"
say Mum and Dad.